I Am the Book

Poems selected by **Lee Bennett Hopkins**

Illustrated by **Yayo**

Holiday House / New York

Contents

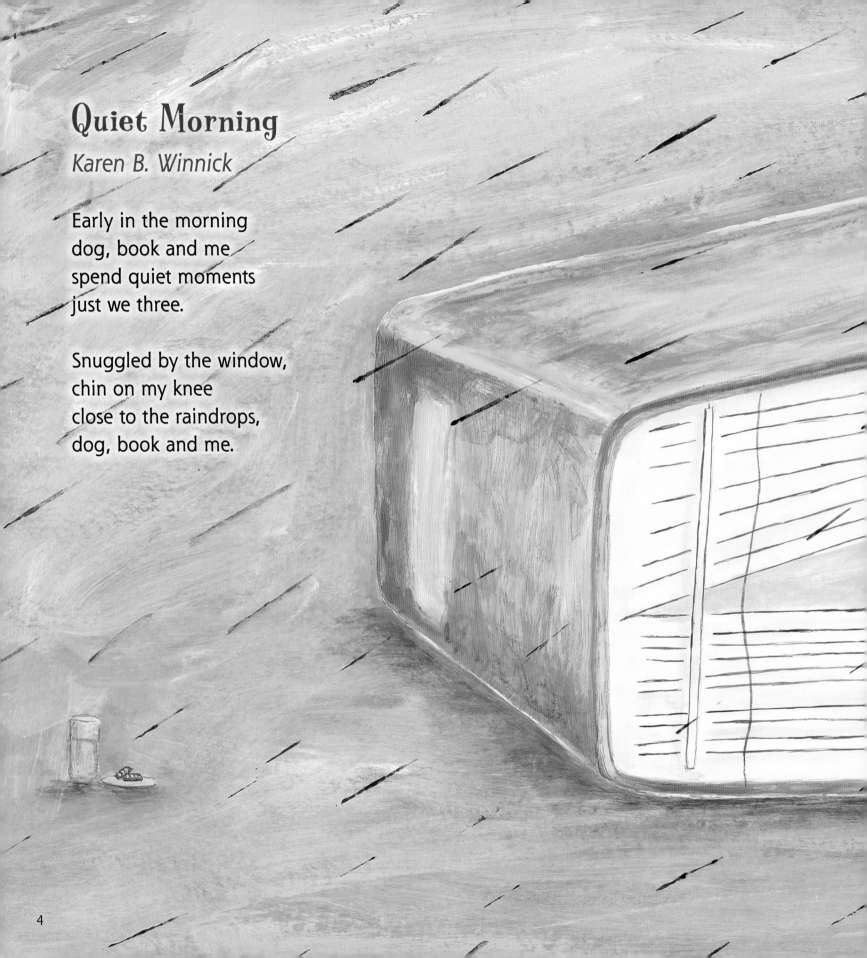

Quiet Morning

Karen B. Winnick

Early in the morning
dog, book and me
spend quiet moments
just we three.

Snuggled by the window,
chin on my knee
close to the raindrops,
dog, book and me.

4

Wonder Through the Pages

Karla Kuskin

So I picked out a book
on my own
from the shelf
and I started to read
on my own
to myself.
And nonsense and knowledge
came tumbling out,
whispering mysteries,
history's shout,
the wisdom of wizards,
the songs of the ages,
all wonders of wandering
wonderful pages.

What Was That?

Rebecca Kai Dotlich

What was that
that made me blink?
Made me wonder,
made me think?

Turned me inside
upside down;
under, over
all around?

What was that
that I just heard?
A treasured tale,
a magic word?

A breathless thought
inside my head—
what was that
that I just read?

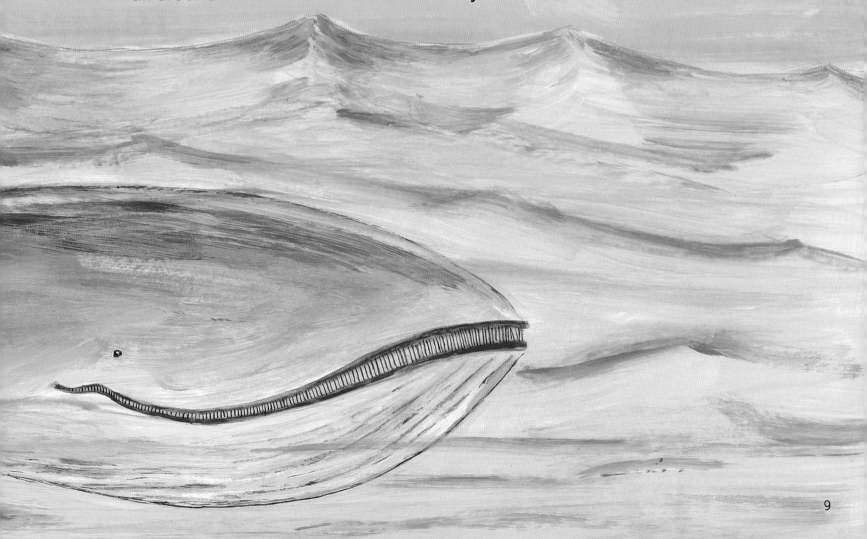

When I Read

Beverly McLoughland

When I read, I like to dive
In the sea of words and swim.
Feet kicking fast across the page
Splashing words against my skin.

When I read, I like to float
Like the gull that trusts the sea,
The ebb and flow of tidal words
Easy under me.

Pirates

Jill Corcoran

Wind whips
    my hair into frayed sails.

Salt water slips
    between my sun-crisped lips.

Gunpowder stabs
    my streaming nostrils.

I storm
    toward shackled screams
    of a kidnapped damsel.

I swashbuckle through my book's
CHAPTER TWO.

Paperback Plunder

Michele Krueger

Like a sunken treasure
long forgotten,
I lie half buried under sand.

She remembered
her sunscreen,
her towel and hat.
She folded her blanket,
and that was that.

No last look back
for what she left behind.

Now I am here
for you to find.

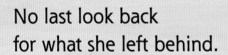

Sun-drenched and salty,
like a giant conch shell.

Lift me to your ear,
Hear the story I shall tell.

Poetry Time

Lee Bennett Hopkins

It's poem o'clock.
Time for a rhyme—

tick-tock
ding-dong
bing-bong
or
chime.

Poems are

wistful
wish-filled
sublime—

Come.

Unlock a minute
for
poetry time.

A Poem Is

Jane Yolen

Words
running
down
the
page,
in black script
sneakers.

Words
nudging/one/another
like bumper cars
at a fair.

Words
humming
thrumming
drumming
strumming
an orchestra
of sounds.

Words that take
a thought,
a wish,
a sentiment,
a prayer,
and then suck out
all the air.

A poem is.

Don't Need a Window Seat

Kristine O'Connell George

Riding home from the library,
don't need a window seat.
Got a great new book to read,
eleven more beneath my feet.

Bus's wheels are turning fast,
I'm starting Chapter One,
hoping I won't reach my stop
before this book is done.

Riding my imagination,
flying down city streets.
Got this great new book to read—
who needs a window seat?

Who's Rich?

Naomi Shihab Nye

Who's rich?
The boy with a book he hasn't read yet.
The girl with a tower of books by her bed.
She opens and opens and opens.
Her life starts everywhere.

Who's rich?
Anyone befriended again & again
by a well-loved book.

This is a wealth
we never lose.

This Book

Avis Harley

This book is the best—
I woke up to read it
Before getting dressed.

This book is so cool—
It's the first thing I grabbed
When I rushed in from school.

This book is a winner—
I forgot I was hungry.
I almost missed dinner.

This book is just right—
I'm reading by flashlight deep into the night
Deliciously thirsty to see how it ends.

Books are such mind-thrilling
Spine-tingling friends.

I Am the Book

Tom Robert Shields

I'll be your friend,
    stay by your side,
    contradict you,
    make you laugh or teary-eyed
On a sun-summer morning.

I'll spark you,
    help you sleep,
    bring dreams
    you'll forever keep
On a dappled-autumn afternoon.

I'll warm you,
    keep you kindled,
    dazzle you
    till storms have dwindled
On a snow-flaked winter evening.

I'll plant in you
    a spring-seedling
    with bursting life
    while you are reading.

I am the book
You are needing.

Book

Amy Ludwig VanDerwater

Buried in blankets
Book in my bed
Snuggled in story
By heart
In my head
I wallow in words
Chapter One
Till The End.

Closing the cover
I sigh—

Good-bye, friend.

About the Poets

Jill Corcoran, a freelance writer, lives in Southern California. "Pirates" is her first poem to appear in an anthology.

Rebecca Kai Dotlich, a prolific poet for children, is also the author of picture books. She lives and works in Carmel, Indiana.

Kristine O'Connell George has received numerous awards for her poetry, including the International Reading Association Lee Bennett Hopkins Promising Poet Award in 1998. She lives in California.

Avis Harley, who lives in Vancouver, British Columbia, has both written and illustrated several books of poetry. She taught elementary school for many years in B.C. and in England.

Lee Bennett Hopkins lives in Cape Coral, Florida. In 2009, he received the National Council of Teachers of English Excellence in Poetry for Children Award.

Michele Krueger works with Young Audiences and California Poets in the Schools, coaching high-school students for the annual national Poetry Out Loud competition. She lives in northern California.

Karla Kuskin is the author-illustrator of more than fifty books. She received the National Council of Teachers of English Excellence in Poetry for Children Award in 1979.

Beverly McLoughland, whose work appears in many anthologies, lives in Williamsburg, Virginia. *A Hippo's A Heap and Other Animal Poems* is her first book of poetry.

Naomi Shihab Nye lives in San Antonio, Texas. Her wide body of work includes *19 Varieties of Gazelle: Poems of the Middle East*, a finalist for the National Book Award.

Tom Robert Shields lived in New York City. His poems appear in several anthologies and are part of educational programs.

Amy Ludwig VanDerwater lives on an old farm in Holland, New York, with her husband and their children. Her work appears in several anthologies.

Karen B. Winnick is the author and illustrator of many picture books, including a book of her poetry, *A Year Goes Round: Poems for the Months*. She lives in California.

Jane Yolen, called the Hans Christian Andersen of America, has written hundreds of books on a wide variety of topics, from science fiction to poetry. She divides her time between Massachusetts and St. Andrews, Scotland.

THANKS ARE DUE TO THE FOLLOWING FOR PERMISSION TO REPRINT THE WORKS LISTED BELOW:

Jill Corcoran for "Pirates." Copyright © 2011 by Jill Corcoran. Used by permission of the author, who controls all rights.

Curtis Brown Ltd. for "What Was That?" by Rebecca Kai Dotlich, copyright © 2011 by Rebecca Kai Dotlich; "Poetry Time" by Lee Bennett Hopkins, copyright © 1992 by Lee Bennett Hopkins; "Quiet Morning" by Karen B. Winnick, copyright © 1998 by Karen B. Winnick; "A Poem Is" by Jane Yolen, copyright © 2004 by Jane Yolen, originally published by The Children's Book Council, Inc. All reprinted by permission of Curtis Brown Ltd.

Avis Harley for "This Book." Copyright © 2011 by Avis Harley. Used by permission of the author, who controls all rights.

Lee Bennett Hopkins for "I Am the Book" by Tom Robert Shields. Copyright © 2011 by Tom Robert Shields. Used by permission of Lee Bennett Hopkins for the author.

Michele Krueger for "Paperback Plunder." Copyright © 2011 by Michele Krueger. Used by permission of the author, who controls all rights.

Beverly McLoughland for "When I Read." Copyright © 2006 by Beverly McLoughland. First appeared in *Teaching Pre K–8*, October 2006. Used by permission of the author, who controls all rights.

Kristine O'Connell George for "Don't Need a Window Seat." Copyright © 2011 by Kristine O'Connell George. Used by permission of the author, who controls all rights.

Naomi Shihab Nye for "Who's Rich?" Copyright © 2011 by Naomi Shihab Nye. Used by permission of the author, who controls all rights.

Scott Treimel NY for "Wonder Through the Pages" by Karla Kuskin from *Moon, Have You Met My Mother?* Copyright © 2003 by Karla Kuskin. Used by permission of Scott Treimel NY.

Amy Ludwig VanDerwater for "Book." Copyright © 2011 by Amy VanDerwater. Used by permission of the author, who controls all rights.

Compilation copyright © 2011 by Lee Bennett Hopkins
Illustrations copyright © 2011 by Diego Herrera (Yayo)
All Rights Reserved
HOLIDAY HOUSE is registered in the U.S. Patent and Trademark Office.
Printed and Bound in October 2010 at Kwong Fat Offset Co., Ltd.,
Dongguan City, Quang Dong Province, China.
The text typeface is Shannon Book.
The artwork was created in acrylics on canvas.
www.holidayhouse.com
First Edition
1 3 5 7 9 10 8 6 4 2

Library of Congress Cataloging-in-Publication Data
I am the book : poems / selected by Lee Bennett Hopkins ; [illustrations by Diego "Yayo" Herrera]. — 1st ed.
p. cm.
ISBN 978-0-8234-2119-0 (hardcover)
1. Books—Juvenile poetry. 2. Books and reading—Juvenile poetry. 3. Children's poetry, American.
I. Hopkins, Lee Bennett. II. Yayo, ill.
PS595.B65132 2011
811'.5408039—dc22
2009014743